New York City, NY

Trenton, NJ

Pittsburgh, PA

Wheeling, WV

Columbus, OH

Dayton, OH

Terre Haute, IN

St. Louis, MO

Carthage, MO

Tulsa, OK

Oklahoma City, OK

Wichita Falls, TX

The HALLELUJAH Flight

Phil Bildner
Illustrated by John Holyfield

G. P. PUTNAM'S SONS ◆ AN IMPRINT OF PENGUIN GROUP (USA) INC.

To Izzy and Lorenzo—
pioneers of the new frontier

P.B.

To my sons, Donovan and Nathaniel,
who bring me joy every day

J.H.

G. P. PUTNAM'S SONS A division of Penguin Young Readers Group. Published by The Penguin Group. Penguin Group (USA) Inc., 375 Hudson Street, New York, NY 10014, U.S.A. Penguin Group (Canada), 90 Eglinton Avenue East, Suite 700, Toronto, Ontario M4P 2Y3, Canada (a division of Pearson Penguin Canada Inc.). Penguin Books Ltd, 80 Strand, London WC2R 0RL, England. Penguin Ireland, 25 St. Stephen's Green, Dublin 2, Ireland (a division of Penguin Books Ltd.). Penguin Group (Australia), 250 Camberwell Road, Camberwell, Victoria 3124, Australia (a division of Pearson Australia Group Pty Ltd). Penguin Books India Pvt Ltd, 11 Community Centre, Panchsheel Park, New Delhi - 110 017, India. Penguin Group (NZ), 67 Apollo Drive, Rosedale, North Shore 0632, New Zealand (a division of Pearson New Zealand Ltd). Penguin Books (South Africa) (Pty) Ltd, 24 Sturdee Avenue, Rosebank, Johannesburg 2196, South Africa. Penguin Books Ltd, Registered Offices: 80 Strand, London WC2R 0RL, England.

Design by Richard Amari. Text set in ITC Cushing. The art was done in acrylics on canvas.

Library of Congress Cataloging-in-Publication Data
Bildner, Phil. The Hallelujah Flight / written by Phil Bildner ; illustrated by John Holyfield.
p. cm. Summary: In 1932, James Banning, along with his co-pilot Thomas Allen, made history by becoming the first African Americans to fly across the United States, relying on the help of people they met in the towns in which they landed along the way, who helped keep their "flying jalopy" going.
1. Banning, James Herman—Juvenile fiction. [1. Banning, James Herman—Fiction. 2. Air pilots—Fiction. 3. Flight—Fiction. 4. African Americans—Fiction.] I. Holyfield, John, ill. II. Title. PZ7.B4923Hal 2010
[E]—dc22 2009010362

ISBN 978-0-399-24789-7
10 9 8 7 6 5 4 3 2 1

A NOTE FROM THE AUTHOR

I first learned of James Banning several years ago when I moved to Brooklyn. In an African-American crafts shop on Dekalb Avenue, I spotted his framed photograph accompanied by a brief paragraph noting his achievements: Banning was the first black aviator to obtain a license from the United States Department of Commerce; he was an ace stunt pilot who starred in scores of aerial shows at the Bessie Coleman Aero Club. And most famously, in 1932, he was the first African American to complete a transcontinental flight.

I was amazed. I taught middle school social studies for over a decade *and* studied American history in college—how could I not have heard of James Banning?

I started researching Banning and was surprised by how little I found other than biographical tidbits and general facts about his historic journey. In time, I did locate two books which provided valuable information and insights—William J. Powell's 1934 *Black Aviator* and Jack Lynn's aptly named 1988 novel, *The Hallelujah Flight*. This latter work was based on news reports, as well as the personal recollections and flight log of Thomas Allen, Banning's mechanic and copilot.

It is through Allen's eyes that I've told this story, and while based on actual events, this picture book should be considered a work of fiction. However, the message here is grounded in truth. James Banning sought to inspire and spur others to act. Perhaps this book will do the same for young readers.

—P. B.

The day I first met James Banning, he said, "Mr. Allen, my dream is to fly a plane from sea to shining sea, and this here OXX6 Eagle Rock is our plane. But first I'll need you to overhaul the engine."

I just about coughed up my coffee. "Replace the entire engine? How will we pay for that?" Times were hard, and most folks didn't have a nickel to spare.

"I've got an idea," Banning replied. "Whenever people give us food, fuel and supplies along the way, they can write their names on the tip of the wing. They'll fly into the history books right along with us!"

"That just might work," I declared.

Banning and I got right down to business fixing our plane.
The crew from the airport thought we'd about lost our
marbles.

"You'll be lucky if you get that crate two inches off the ground!" cried the carpenter.

"Even luckier if it lasts two minutes in the air!" echoed the engineer.

"They're a pair of hoboes," mocked the mechanic.

"The Flying Hoboes!" they all called us.

Nevertheless, on the afternoon of
September 19, 1932, we Flying Hoboes
climbed into the cramped cockpits
of the OXX6 Eagle Rock and took off
from Dycer Airport on the outskirts
of Los Angeles.

"Here we go!" Banning cried.

What a racket it made! The engine whined, my fittings creaked and the tail section rattled.

On top of that, our plane seemed to have a mind all its own. Without any warning, it rocketed into a rise and then shot down into a dive. It kept us on our toes hundreds of feet in the air!

That first day we didn't even make it out of California. Then again, we weren't really expecting to. We just wanted to be sure our plane could fly.

When we landed after the first leg of the trip,
I inspected our plane from nose to tail.

"We have a leaky pump," I said. "I'm going to
need some tools and parts. It's time we put your
plan to the test."

Banning and I headed into town and asked for help. At first, like the airport workers, the locals thought we were missing a few screws. However, as soon as we told them they could sign their names on the wing, every last one of them pitched in to help.

Bright and early the next morning, we headed on our way. Flying over the desert of southern California, the cozy cockpits heated up like ovens.

"It's too hot," I yelled.

"Do what I do," Banning hollered back.

Suddenly, Banning was unhooking his overalls and unbuttoning his shirt. In a matter of moments, the two of us were flying in nothing but our underwear!

The next leg of our journey took us Flying Hoboes over the state of Arizona. We soared high above the Grand Canyon, the Painted Desert and the Petrified Forest.

As nightfall neared, Banning spotted a familiar airfield in the distance.

In the dark, Banning made his approach. He banked us around a group of mountains, and after almost sideswiping a silo, he slammed the plane down on the runway.

The moment my feet touched the good earth, I cried, "Hallelujah!"

"Hallelujah right back at you!" Banning replied.

The airport manager greeted us. "Hey, ain't you that fella who blew out them tires landin' here some time ago?"

"Perhaps," Banning answered cautiously. "Why do you ask?"

"Well, I'll be!" the manager yelled. "Thanks to that lil' accident of yers, the city built us this brand spankin' new runway! How can we ever repay you?"

Banning's face lit up like a lightbulb. "Well, we'd be honored if you would sign the tip of our wing. And for good measure, how about sending us off with some food and gasoline?"

The next day, we were back on our way. However, as we headed on east, we encountered something far more dangerous than hot weather and nightfall:

Prejudice.

At one stop, all we wanted was to use a washroom.

"Climb back into that contraption of yours," the airport supervisor barked, "and go back to where you came from!"

At another stop, we wandered into town to find some food.

"We don't serve your kind around here," the waiter growled.

"You ain't good 'nough for our eats."

We turned tail and flew off for our lives.

"Hallelujah!" I said when the plane's wheels lifted off the dirt.

"Hallelujah right back at you!" Banning replied.

Our fortunes turned in Oklahoma, where we were able to rely on the kindness of family and friends.

"Y'all look like you need some clean clothes and a warm bath," Mama Allen said when we stopped in Oklahoma City. "I smelled y'all before you crossed the state line."

"Here are some fresh vegetables," said my high school sweetheart. "You boys need to stay healthy up there."

"Take these plugs from my plow," said Banning's brother in El Reno.
"In case you get any more leaks."

"And here are some sandwiches," said his cousin. "I'll make as many
as you can fit."

Of course, they all signed their names to the wing of our flying jalopy.

From Springfield, Illinois, to Terre Haute, Indiana, to Columbus, Ohio, we flew without problems. But heading into Pittsburgh, we ran into a ferocious storm, the worst one of the entire journey.

"We're going down!" Banning cried as he pulled up on the throttle to avoid a cluster of trees.

"But where's the airfield?" I shouted.

"Airfield? I'm aiming for that wheat field!"

On the landing, both wings buckled and part of the nose fell off. But somehow, we made it down in one piece.

"Hallelujah," I told my pilot and friend.

"Hallelujah right back at you," he replied.

"Rise and shine," Banning said the next morning with the first signs of light. "I can almost taste the salt of the Atlantic Ocean!"

We jostled by Johnstown, hiccupped past Harrisburg and dipped over the Delaware before finally landing at Mercer Airport in West Trenton, New Jersey.

After 3,300 miles and 21 days, we had just one small hop to go.

On Sunday morning, October 9, 1932, James Banning piloted our OXX6 Eagle Rock over New York Harbor. We saluted the Statue of Liberty before turning toward Valley Stream Airport in Long Island, New York.

"Hallelujah!" I cried.

"Hallelujah right back at you!" Banning replied for the final time.

We received a hero's welcome in Harlem. A banquet dinner was held in our honor, and hundreds lined the streets just to shake our hands.

"You call yourselves the Flying Hoboes," a reporter called out as we greeted the throngs, "but have you got a name for this adventure?"

We grabbed hands and raised our arms to the heavens.
"The Hallelujah Flight!"

The HALLELUJAH Flight

Los Angeles, CA

Yuma, AZ

Lordsburg, NM

Midland, TX

Tucson, AZ

El Paso, TX